NOBODY KNOWS

Written by A. Shelton Rollins
Illustrated by Pamela Carthorn
Book Design by Solid Rox Media, Inc.

LIFT EVERY VOICE / CHICAGO

LIFT EVERY VOICE / CHICAGO

A Division of Moody Publishers
820 N. La Salle Boulevard
Chicago, Illinois 60610-3284

First published in 2003 by Lift Every Voice
Copyright © A. Shelton Rollins, 2003
Illustrations copyright © Pamela Carthorn, 2003

ISBN 0-8024-2920-3

Printed in Italy

DEDICATIONS

For Adina and Elvin, my great-grandmothers, my husband, and my Lord, Jesus Christ.

— A. Shelton Rollins

To my awesome God who continues to love me.
To my son, Shannon; my daughters, Oreanna, Victoria and Tatianna.
To their grandparents, Grandma Moore and Great-Grandma Taylor.
To my parents, Eddie and Glorene Epps.
I love you all.

Thank you for all your support and encouragement.

— Love, Pamm

The Negro National Anthem

Lift every voice and sing
Till earth and heaven ring,
Ring with the harmonies of Liberty;
Let our rejoicing rise
High as the listening skies,
Let it resound loud as the rolling sea.
Sing a song, full of the faith that the dark past has taught us,
Sing a song, full of the hope that the present has brought us,
Facing the rising sun, of our new day begun
Let us march on till victory is won.

So begins the Black National Anthem, by James Weldon Johnson, in 1900. Lift Every Voice is the name of the joint imprint of The Institute for Black Family Development and Moody Publishers, a division of the Moody Bible Institute.

Our vision is to advance the cause of Christ through publishing African-American Christians who educate, edify, and disciple Christians in the church community through quality books written for African-Americans.

The Institute for Black Family Development is a national Christian organization. It offers degreed and non-degreed training nationally and internationally to established and emerging leaders from churches and Christian organizations. To learn more about The Institute for Black Family Development, write us at:

The Institute for Black Family Development
15151 Faust
Detroit, MI 48223

Eran was like most eight-year-old boys. He liked to play with his cars and trucks and play most any game. He even liked his baby sister . . . sometimes . . . and himself . . . usually.

He liked his deep, chocolate skin, until someone asked why his was darker. He liked his sun-kissed, raisin-brown eyes, until someone asked why his weren't blue. He liked his bumpy, black-licorice curls, until someone touched them—again.

Sometimes he just felt so different—and not the good kind of different, like the way you feel at your birthday party, he felt the bad kind of different—especially when he went to school and heard about African people, who looked like him, being made into slaves.

That's why Eran loved spending every summer at MawMaw and Grandpa's farm. There he could forget that "different" feeling.

There Grandpa's hardened hands—brown-black and strong from long years of hard work—could tenderly hold the smallest baby chick for Eran to inspect.

There MawMaw—gingersnap brown and thin, with a sweetness and an in-charge spiciness—directed every detail of life on the farm.

There. That's where Eran loved to be.

One warm summer night, as Eran sat eating MawMaw's hand-cranked ice cream, MawMaw made a surprising announcement: "Tomorrow's the big Juneteenth celebration in town. We're going," she said with unusual excitement, "to celebrate when the slaves were freed."

The people are informed that in accordance with a Proclamation from the Executive of the United States, all slaves are free... absolute... freed are advised to remain at their present homes, and work for wages. They are informed that they will not be allowed... at military...

The people are informed that

Eran suddenly felt sick with that bad feeling of different.

"What's wrong with you, son?" MawMaw asked, pressing her warm palm against his forehead. "You get on to bed, and I'll bring something to fix you right up."

Eran slowly stood up and walked to his room.

7

When MawMaw came in with the tall bottle of medicine and spoon, Eran took a deep breath and asked, "MawMaw, do I have to go to the Juneteenth thing? Can I please stay home?"

"Of course it's not okay," said MawMaw in a huff. "You'll get to play with the boys, and I know you love to sing and watch fireworks, and . . ." MawMaw stopped midsentence and looked closely at Eran's sad eyes. "What's wrong?" she said slowly. "Don't you want to celebrate the freeing of the slaves?"

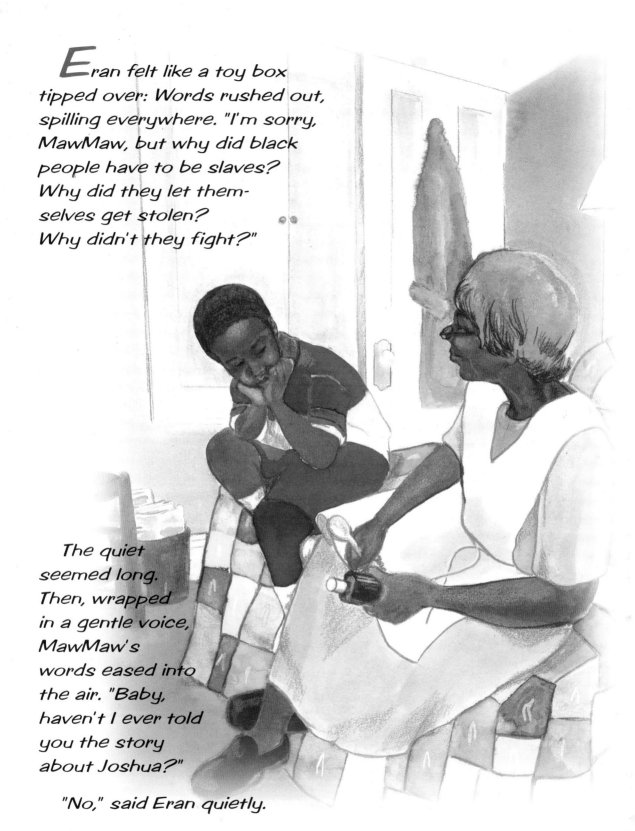

*E*ran felt like a toy box
tipped over: Words rushed out,
spilling everywhere. "I'm sorry,
MawMaw, but why did black
people have to be slaves?
Why did they let them-
selves get stolen?
Why didn't they fight?"

The quiet
seemed long.
Then, wrapped
in a gentle voice,
MawMaw's
words eased into
the air. "Baby,
haven't I ever told
you the story
about Joshua?"

"No," said Eran quietly.

So MawMaw sat next to Eran and began her story.

Joshua was a slave boy," MawMaw began. "He probably looked a bit like you, but his skin was darker: the color of good, rich dirt. The kind you just know is going to grow something good.

"When Joshua was your age, he worked in the big house where the slave owner and his family lived. His job was to help the owner's wife. Sometimes he would get things she needed or help her with her sewing."

Well, one day, while Joshua was helping her, he saw the children learning to read. He thought that was some sort of magic—looking at those books with white sheets and speaking words—so one time when their mama wasn't around, Joshua asked the children to teach him the magic. But they just laughed and said he could never read.

"That night, Joshua asked his grandmother why they thought he couldn't read. 'Child,' she said, 'some people think they can treat us like less than people just because we look and talk different than they do. But the Bible says it doesn't matter how we look, or whether we are slaves or free people. God says we are all made special.

You know, people said Jesus wasn't anybody,' she continued, 'but they were wrong. He was God's very own Son, and He wants you to bring your troubles to Him because He understands.'

"And she began to sing:

"'Nobody knows the trouble I've seen.

Nobody knows but Jesus.

Nobody knows the trouble I've seen.

Glory hallelujah!

"'Now, learning to read,' Grandma paused, 'they could kill you for that. But you take that problem to Jesus, child. God sent Jesus to do something special, and He made you special because He wants you to do something special, too. And He'll help you do it if you trust Him.'

Well, Joshua did what his grandmother said. He took his problem to Jesus, and he asked God if it would be all right for him to learn to read. And do you know what? Joshua did learn. He read the Bible and its stories, like the one about the great African man named Nimrod.

"And years later, when the slaves were freed, Joshua started a school to teach their children to read. He found the special something that God made for him to do."

MawMaw paused and looked deep into Eran's eyes, as if she were trying to plant something there. Finally, she said, "Never let someone else tell you who you are. God says we are all wonderfully made. You are special, and God has something special for you to do."

Eran was quiet. He understood now. "Thank you, MawMaw," said Eran, slowly. "And, MawMaw," he said with a smile, "what time do we leave tomorrow?"

"Right after morning chores," replied MawMaw. She kissed Eran's cheek—something she seldom did— and then with spicy-crispness added, "Get some sleep." With the brown bottle and spoon still in her hands, she rose and left the room.

*B*efore he said his prayers that night, Eran thought about Joshua. He'd found a way to fight the bad feeling of different and do something special, because he was special.

Eran climbed out of bed and stood in front of the long mirror that hung on the back of the bedroom door. He looked at his deep chocolate skin, raisin-brown eyes, and black-licorice curls. Then Eran did something he hadn't done in a long time—he smiled at himself!

Down the hall, he could hear MawMaw's voice, still singing,

"Nobody knows the trouble I've seen.
Nobody knows but Jesus.
Nobody knows the trouble I've seen.
Glory hallelujah!"

SCRIPTURES

There is neither . . . slave nor free . . . for you are all one in Christ Jesus. *(Galatians 3:28)*

Jesus . . . came into His hometown . . . . *[and]* began to teach in the synagogue; and the many listeners were astonished, saying, "Where did this man get these things?. . . . Is not this the carpenter?" *(Mark 6:1-3)*

I will instruct you and teach you in the way which you should go; I will counsel you with My eye upon you. *(Psalm 32:8)*

I can do all things through Him who strengthens me. *(Philippians 4:13)*

Cush became the father of Nimrod; he became a mighty one on the earth. He was a mighty hunter before the Lord; therefore it is said, "Like Nimrod a mighty hunter before the Lord." *(Genesis 10:8-9)*

I will give thanks to You, for I am fearfully and wonderfully made; wonderful are Your works, and my soul knows it very well. *(Psalm 139:14)*

Casting all your anxiety on Him, because He cares for you. *(I Peter 5:7)*